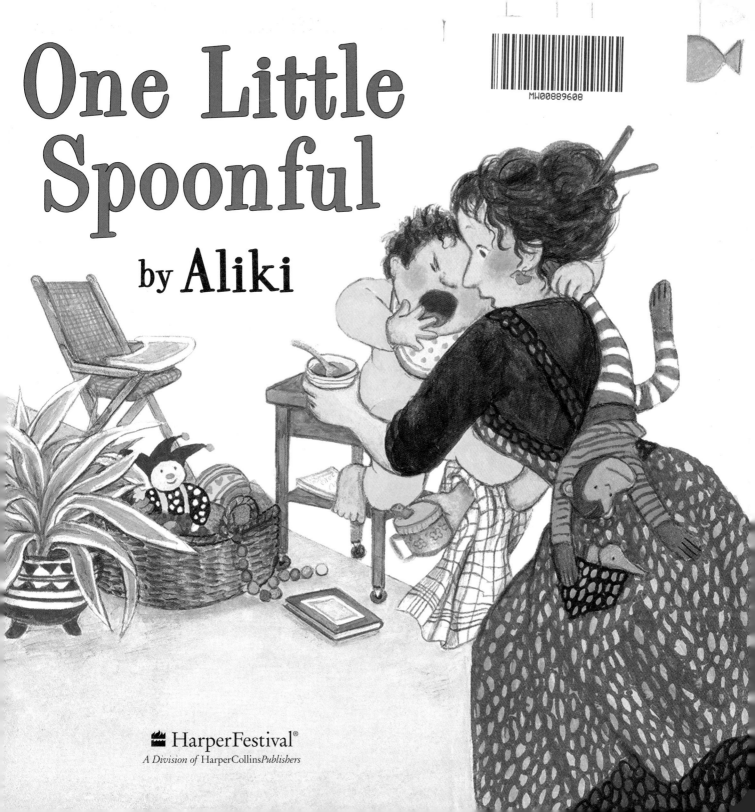

One Little Spoonful

by Aliki

HarperFestival®
A Division of HarperCollinsPublishers

One little spoonful
for your toes.

One little spoonful
for your nose.

One little taste
for a hungry tum.

Open the door,
and down it goes.
YUM!

One little sip
for your fingers and eyes.

Close them
and taste one more
spoonful surprise.

Wipe it all up,
and there's one more to go.

Last little spoonful.

Now what do you say?

Now let's go and play.